D0960289

Clara Lee
and the
Apple Pie Dream

Clara Lee

and the

Apple Pie Dream

Jenny Han

with pictures by Julia Kuo

LITTLE, BROWN AND COMPANY
New York   Boston

Little, Brown and Company

Hachette Book Group
237 Park Avenue, New York, NY 10017
Visit our website at www.lb-kids.com

Little, Brown and Company is a division of Hachette Book Group, Inc.
The Little, Brown name and logo are trademarks of Hachette Book Group, Inc.

First Edition: January 2011

The characters and events portrayed in this book are fictitious. Any similarity to
real persons, living or dead, is coincidental and not intended by the author.

Library of Congress Cataloging-in-Publication Data
Han, Jenny.
Clara Lee and the apple pie dream / by Jenny Han ; illustrations by Julia Kuo.
— 1st ed.   p. cm.
Summary: Korean American fourth-grader Clara Lee longs to be Little Miss
Apple Pie, and when her luck seems suddenly to change for the better, she
overcomes her fear of public speaking and enters the competition.
ISBN 978-0-316-07038-6
[1. Luck—Fiction. 2. Schools—Fiction. 3. Family life—Fiction.
4. Korean Americans—Fiction.] I. Kuo, Julia, ill. II. Title.
PZ7.H18944Cl 2011
[Fic] —dc22
2010006900

10 9 8 7 6 5 4 3 2 1

RRD-C

Printed in the United States of America

For my Grandpa, from your best girl —J.H.

To Mom, Dad, and Susie Lee —J.K.

Clara Lee
and the
Apple Pie Dream

CHAPTER 1

When I woke up that morning and saw the red and gold leaves swirling around my backyard, I just knew it was gonna be my kind of day. We started collecting leaves early in the morning, and by afternoon, we had three very

1

nice, fat piles. My best friend, Shayna; my little sister, Emmeline; and me, Clara Lee. Clara Lee is my name, first and last. All the kids at school call me Clara Lee and not just Clara. It just sounds better that way. Like peanut butter and jelly, like trick-or-treat, or fairy and princess, those words just go together. Just like me, Clara Lee.

Later on, we would jump in our leaf piles, but first, we were playing a game I made up called Fall Royalty. Shayna is Queen, Emmeline is Prince, and I am the King of Fall.

"Why do you always get to be king?" Emmeline complained. She loves to complain; it's her favorite hobby. She is six. She's small for her age. A runt, like Wilbur from *Charlotte's Web*. I call her that when no one's listening. It really makes her mad. She has chubby cheeks and round button eyes and everybody thinks she is just the cutest thing ever. But not me. I can see through her like plastic wrap.

"It's not fair," she whined.

"I'm the one who made up the game," I reminded her. "If you don't want to play, you can go and help Grandpa—"

Emmeline pushed her bottom lip out a smidge but didn't argue. She scooped another leaf off the ground and added it to her pile.

I picked a brownish leaf out of the pile. "Not bright enough," I declared, in my best King of Fall voice.

Emmeline put her hands on her hips. "Just because you're the king—," she started to say. Then she looked over at Shayna. "Shayna, do you think it's fair that Clara Lee gets to be king?"

"I would rather be queen any day," Shayna said, fixing her crown of leaves so it set just

3

right on her head. "Why don't you be princess instead of prince this time?"

"Princesses are boring," Emmeline said. And then she threw her handful of leaves in the air and danced around our pile. She bounced around like a kangaroo, shook her hips from side to side, and moved her arms like she was doing the backstroke.

Shayna and I looked at each other and shrugged. And then we threw our leaves in the air too, and we danced like Emmeline danced.

After all the dancing, it was time for me to make my toast to fall. I had already practiced it that morning when I brushed my teeth. "Ahem. Now the king will make a toast." I paused dramatically. I lifted the jug of apple cider that my mom had brought out for us.

"A toast? But we already had breakfast," Emmeline whispered to Shayna.

"A toast is a speech," Shayna explained.

"Then why didn't she just say speech?"

"Quiet, the both of you!" I boomed. Shayna glared at me, and I mouthed, *Sorry*. Then I cleared my throat. "Fall is a time of change. The seasons are changing. Soon it will be cold. But we will always, always remember the fall, because it is the best time of year. Amen."

Emmeline crossed her eyes at me. She learned that talent very recently, and now she does it every opportunity she gets, because she knows I can't. Emmeline said, "I like summer the best."

"Do not disrespect fall," I told her, taking a swig from the jug. Then I passed it to Shayna, who sipped it in her ladylike way. Then she passed it to Emmeline, who drank almost half of it.

Our leaf piles were looking good, so I said, "Ready?"

Shayna and Emmeline yelled, "Ready!"

We all jumped into our piles at the same time. It was like jumping into a cloud of fall. Leaves floated in the air like snowflakes. We three couldn't stop screaming, it was so fun.

After a lot of jumping, we laid down on our leaf piles. It was getting dark. We would have to go inside soon. That was the only bad thing about fall. It got dark so darned quick.

"Clara Lee?" Shayna's leaf pile was in the middle, right in between Emmeline and me.

"Yeah?"

"Apple Blossom Festival is coming up really soon. Are you going to try out for Little Miss Apple Pie?"

"I don't know. Haven't even thought about it," I lied.

"That's a lie, Clara Lee!" said Emmeline. "I saw you practicing your wave yesterday."

I told her, "You shouldn't spy on people."

She was right though. I'd thought about it plenty.

CHAPTER 2

Apple Blossom Festival was right around the corner. It was always at the beginning of October. It kicks off the whole holiday season. We've got Apple Blossom Festival, then

Halloween, then Thanksgiving, then Christmas. We're so lucky.

I'd say Apple Blossom Festival is a pretty big deal in Bramley. There's apple bobbing in the town square, and at the booths, they've got caramel apples and candy apples and just about every kind of apple you can think of. Plenty of Bramley Seedlings, which is what our town is named for.

One of my favorite things is the apple dessert contest. Usually it's good stuff, like Mrs. Kollmann's German apple cake, and apple turnovers, and apple cider doughnuts. Last year, Mrs. Novak made an apple pie with a cheddar cheese whipped cream, and it made me nervous on apple pie. Grandpa liked it though. He even had seconds. I think he was the only person in the whole town who had seconds on that cheesy pie.

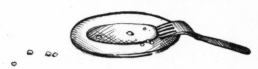

There's even a parade, with floats. Only Very Important People get to ride on the floats. Like Mr. Cooper who owns Cooper's Drugstore, he has a float. The YMCA has a float. The mayor is on a float. The firemen too. But most important of all is Miss Apple Pie and Little Miss Apple Pie.

Miss Apple Pie is pretty much a dream come true. Only when you're a high school girl can you be Miss Apple Pie; the whole high school votes on who gets to be her. You wear a red sash and a tiara with little red apples on top. You wave, and you throw apple

candy at the crowd. Everyone cheers for you. Little Miss Apple Pie gets to stand next to her and hold the bag of candy. She gets to wear a sash too, and a tiara that is less fancy but still beautiful.

Last year, Trudie Turner from the fifth grade was Little Miss Apple Pie. Since I'm only in the third grade, I don't know her, but she looked pretty good up there on the float. Her hair was curled and tied back with red ribbon. Miss Apple Pie was a high school girl with long blonde hair and she wore a red dress and red high heels. She looked like a girl in a commercial.

If I won, I knew just what I'd wear. The dress Grandpa bought me in Korea last year. It's Korean style, with a skirt the color of fruit punch and a white jacket with rainbow-striped sleeves and, best of all, a long bow. I've only ever worn it on New Year's Day, and I felt like a Korean princess from long ago. Emmeline has one too, but hers is a navy jacket. I could almost picture it: me, in my Korean dress, on that float.

The way you get chosen is this: You make a speech during a special assembly in front of the whole school. Even if you're only a second grader, you have to compete against the fifth graders. It's the rules. Last year, I was too scared to make a speech. Getting up in front of everybody and making a speech just isn't my cup of cocoa. I wanted to win Little Miss Apple Pie so, so bad, but it was that darned speech that held me back. I'm brave in other ways, like I always jump off the high dive at the pool, not the baby dive. I'm not scared to raise my hand and answer questions in class. In fact, I love it. But speaking up in class is not the same thing as making a speech in front of the whole school. It's not the same at all.

CHAPTER 3

When it started to get not just a little but a lot dark, Grandpa called us in for dinner. "Clara-yah," he called. "Emma-yah! Time for dinner." In Korean, adding the "yah" when you're talking to somebody is kind of like saying, Hey there, Clara. I know hardly any Korean, but I know about that.

For dinner, we had chicken soup with lots of garlic and ginseng root. Mom made it. She served it up with her big silver ladle. "Eat up," she said, and her glasses were foggy from the hot soup.

Emmeline took one look at her bowl and said, "What's this tree doing in my soup?"

I could tell Daddy was trying not to smile. He has dimples that always peek out even when he tries to hide them. He said, "Em, it's not a tree. It's ginseng and it's good for you. Tasty too!"

"Ginseng is like medicine. Very powerful," said Grandpa, picking up his bowl and drinking from it. "Keep the doctor away."

"It smells weird," said Emmeline.

"No, it doesn't, you've had it before bunches of times," I told her.

"I have?"

"Yeah, and you loved it."

"I did?"

"Yeah," I said.

I'll do anything to keep the doctor away, so I ate two bowls. Plus, it's yummo. Emmeline only ate it after Daddy put in a bunch of hot sauce so her soup was bright red.

After dinner, my mom quizzed me on my multiplication tables while Emmeline colored harvest fruits and vegetables on her worksheets. It looked fun. Way funner than math.

When we were on the sixes, I said, "Why does Emmeline get to color while I have to do math?"

"Coloring is her homework," my mom said, looking over at Emmeline. "When you were little, your homework was coloring too, you know."

"I don't think coloring should count as homework," I said. Emmeline looked up at me and smiled a sneaky little smile. I ignored her. "Where's Grandpa, anyway? We were going to read together."

My mom yawned. "He went to sleep early. He overdid it in the garden today. Now, six times seven."

"Forty-two. What do you mean, overdid it? Is Grandpa sick?"

"No, buddy. He's just getting older. When you get older, your body gets a little creaky, that's all."

My mom calls me buddy when she's loving me especially much. She calls me kid when she's loving me not so much. Some days, I walk a fine line between buddy and kid. But that night, I was buddy.

I snuggled in closer to her. In a little voice, I asked her, "Is Grandpa really old?"

"No way, buddy," said my mom. "He's a tough guy. He's gonna be with us for a long time."

"What do you consider a long time?" I asked her.

"What do *you* consider a long time?" she asked me right back.

I thought it over. "Six years," I said. Six years was how old Emmeline was. She'd been getting on my nerves for six whole years. In my opinion, six years was a long time.

"Well, then I think Grandpa is going to be here for a long, long time," my mom told me. "Now, seven times eight."

I could tell my mom was telling the truth, the way her voice was steady and the way she looked me right in the eyes. I have a talent for lie detection. I am a lie detective.

That night, I dreamed about the Mustache Man. I dream about him every once in a while, ever since I was little. We know each other well, but trust me when I say he's no friend of mine. The Mustache Man is a cartoon man with a huge

head and a huge mustache and he chases me around with a big can of bug spray. He is a truly frightening fellow.

This time, Grandpa and I were walking to the barber shop, and then, suddenly, the Mustache Man was coming behind us in a chariot. "Clara Leeee," he called. Grandpa and I held hands and tried to run, but because of Grandpa's bad leg, we couldn't run fast enough. The Mustache Man caught up with us. He sprayed his big can of magical bug spray in Grandpa's face, and Grandpa started coughing and then he fell right over. I shook him and shook him, but he wouldn't wake up. The Mustache Man's magic was just too strong.

When I woke up, I could still smell the bug spray. I was so scared I almost ran to my mom and dad's room. But seeing as how I'm eight now, it didn't seem right.

Instead, I woke up my sister, Emmeline. Emmeline and I have a bunk bed. She is on top, I am on bottom.

I called out, "Emmeline, are you awake?" knowing full well she wasn't.

She didn't answer, so I said, in an even louder voice, "Emmeline, are you awake? Wake up! I just had the worst dream of my life!" And then I climbed up to her bunk and poked her in the back until she woke up. When she finally did, I told her all about my dream. About how the Mustache Man had a curly brown mustache and how he wore overalls and how he had pretzel breath. How he finally caught up with Grandpa and me and sprayed Grandpa with his poison.

"In my dream, Grandpa didn't look so good." I didn't want to scare her, but she had to know.

She said, "Grandpa looks fine to me. And anyway, I like pretzels and I *like* scary dreams."

I said, "No you do not. Nobody likes scary dreams."

"*I* do. I like being scared. Scary movies are my favorite thing."

"You're not even allowed to watch scary movies!" By that time, I wasn't even scared anymore. I was *annoyed* because my sister can be very *annoying*.

"That's why I like scary dreams. They're like a movie, but better, because *I'm* the star."

And then we played thumb war until we got sleepy again.

CHAPTER 4

Whenever I have an interesting, scary, or fabulous dream, I tell Grandpa about it the next morning. It's because my grandpa is a dream genius. He knows what it all means; he can make sense of anything. That's because he comes from Korea, where they know all about those kind of things.

I am Korean American, which means I was born in America but my blood is Korean, so those secrets are inside me too. They're just hidden real deep so I can't always get to them. But Grandpa can, and he's teaching me how. One day, I'll be as good as him. Better, even. Grandpa says that because I am a girl I am more in touch with this kind of thing. He says that in Korea, women used to speak to gods and spirits, and people would pay them money to hear what they thought about things. They were called shamans, and everybody listened to them and gave them lots of respect. That sounds pretty good to me!

I wanted to tell Grandpa about my Mustache

Man dream, but I was worried I'd scare him. So I made up my mind not to say a word about it.

Trust Emmeline to mess things up as usual. The next morning at breakfast, she said, "Aren't you going to tell Grandpa about your dream, Clara Lee?"

I glared at her. "Mind your own beeswax."

"But you always tell Grandpa about your dreams," she said.

"Clara, you had a dream last night?" Grandpa asked, sitting down next to me.

Instead of answering him, I said, "Um. Will you braid my hair in the French way, Grandpa?"

He said, "Shore, Clara. No problem." And then, like he was a mind reader, he said, "So. Tell me about your dream."

I didn't know what to say. I didn't want to

scare him. So instead, I said, "Did Daddy eat all the Rice Krispies, Grandpa?"

"Yes. You can have Trix." Grandpa passed me the cereal box. "Clara-yah, why you don't tell me about your dream?"

I bit my lip. "Because, Grandpa, it was too terrible."

"Terrible?" Grandpa perked up. "Tell me more."

I shook my head. "I can't. It's too terrible to repeat."

"Repeat? What you mean, repeat?"

"It means to say again," I explained.

"Ohhh. Repeat! I know repeat. So repeat, Clara-yah. Tell me!"

"Fine, but don't say I didn't warn you," I said, pouring some cereal into my favorite bunny bowl. "You were in my dream, Grandpa."

"I was? Tell me more."

"In my dream, we were walking to the barber. You know, the one by church?"

"Yeah yeah, I know the one," he said.

"Well, we were walking, and then...the Mustache Man came after us in a chariot—"

"What is cherry-it?"

Hmm. How to describe a chariot? I said, "You know those wagons that are pulled by horses? Like in Egypt, in the Bible?"

"Ahh. Spell it, please." Grandpa whipped out the little red notebook and pen he keeps in his shirt pocket. He likes to write down words he doesn't know and look them up later with his special Korean dictionary.

"C-H-A-R-I—" I hesitated. "E-T."

Grandpa jotted it down and said, "So? Keep on telling your dream."

I sighed. "So, we were walking to the barber, and the Mustache Man came after us in a chariot, and he caught up with us. And he took out his big can of bug spray and he sprayed you right in the face...."

"And?" He leaned forward eagerly.

I whispered, "And then you fell asleep and you wouldn't wake up."

Grandpa clapped his hands together. "That's a good dream, Clara-yah! Don't you know?"

I couldn't believe it. "No I *don't* know!" I said. "What I do know is that it was so scary that when I woke up, I *still* felt scared. That is not what I call a good dream."

"Ah, Clara-yah, but death in a dream means change. Good change. It's Good Luck."

I perked right up. "Really?" I asked him. "Really, really?"

"Oh yeah," he said, nodding knowingly. "You gonna have some Good Luck coming your way, you'll see. Maybe Grandpa will buy a lottery ticket today. I gonna use my Clara's birthday numbers."

Wow. I leaned back in my chair and let out a big breath. My day was off to some kind of start.

Then Emmeline said, "You wanna hear *my* dream, Grandpa?"

"Shore, shore, of course I do," he said.

"I dreamed that I was a king and everybody was bowing down to me," she announced, giving me a superior kind of look.

I snorted and said, "Emmeline, you only had that dream because we learned about Joseph and his coat at Sunday school last week.

Remember how Joseph had that dream where his brothers were bowing down to him?"

Emmeline sniffed. "Yeah, and remember how Joseph really did become king and his brothers really did bow down to him?"

"No, but I remember that his brothers sold him into slavery for being so very *obnoxious*," I said. I doubted she even knew what obnoxious meant.

Emmeline stuck her tongue out at me. "Bow down to me, brother!" she shouted. That's when Daddy came into the kitchen and said, "What's this I hear about bowing and selling somebody into slavery?"

"Nothing," I muttered.

Emmeline mouthed, *Bow down, brother.*

I raised my hand to give her a good pinch, but Grandpa stopped me in the nick of time.

He said, "Emmeline has big dream because she is a big spirit. Just like a dragon to have a dream like that."

"Did you hear that, Daddy? I am a big spirit," she said with her mouth full of kimchi. She likes kimchi for breakfast, and she likes it for lunch, and she likes it for dinner. It's peppery cabbage and it gives her spicy breath, but she doesn't even care.

"You're also a big pain in the you-know-what," I muttered. She thinks she's hot stuff because she's a dragon and I'm a cow. In the Chinese zodiac, there is an animal for every year, twelve in all. We're not Chinese, we're Korean, but Korean people still follow it. I was born in the Year of the Cow, which means I am hardworking and determined. Emmeline was born in the Year of the Dragon, the so-called mightiest sign of all.

Daddy and Emmeline didn't hear me, but Grandpa did. "Not nice, Clara," he said with a shake of his head.

Whoops. I hate it when Grandpa catches me in the act. I hunched my shoulders down and finished my Trix.

Then my mom came into the kitchen all dressed for work and said, "Appa, don't forget to do your leg exercises today."

"Appa" means "Daddy" in Korean, so that's what Mom calls Grandpa because he is her dad. Sometimes I call my daddy Appa or my mom

Uhmma, but only on special occasions like when I'm in trouble or I want something really badly. In Korean, everyone has a special name. I'm Uhnee because that means "big sister." In Korea, everybody who is a big sister is called Uhnee. It's like a big-sister club. But even though I am in that club, Emmeline almost never calls me Uhnee. Even though she is supposed to.

Grandpa said, "Gina, I need you to take me to 7-Eleven today."

"For what?" Mom looked suspicious.

"Appa gotta pick up something," Grandpa said.

"What do you need? I'll get it for you."

"I gotta pick up Mega Millions lottery ticket," Grandpa said. He winked at me, and I winked back.

"Appa, I don't think you should waste your

36

money on lottery tickets," Mom said, shaking her head.

"Not waste," Grandpa said, giving her a stern look. "Anyway, it's Appa's money."

Mom sighed and Daddy said, "Dad, I'll pick you up a ticket on the way home from work."

"I write down numbers for you," Grandpa said, pulling out his little notebook again. "We feel lucky today."

Grandpa raised his hand and we high-fived. I felt lucky already.

CHAPTER 5

On Bus Number 19, this is how we sit: Shayna and me in one seat and Georgina and Max in the seat behind us. We sit like that every day, so long as one of us isn't in a fight with the other. If we are in a fight, we switch: me and Georgina, Shayna and Max. Or me and Max, Shayna and Georgina.

Besides Shayna, Max and Georgina are my best friends. The two of them look alike; they both have light blond hair and brown eyes. I guess it makes sense, seeing as how they are twins and all. They might look the same, but they are pretty different. Georgina collects bottle caps and she loves baseball. Max likes science, and he has a fancy laboratory set that he lets us play with sometimes. Also, Max does ballet, and Georgina does tae kwon do. Still, the two of them are two peas in a pod.

When Shayna and I got on the bus, Georgina and Max were sitting in the seat in the way back. The seat in the back of the bus is the best seat on the whole bus! It is superlong and a little bit bouncy and everyone always wants to sit there. But of course, it's always the fifth

graders who get to sit back there because they're the oldest.

Shayna and I slid into the seat in front of them. "How'd you guys get this seat?" Shayna wanted to know.

"The fifth graders have their field trip to the dump today," said Georgina.

"Lucky ducks," I said.

Max said, "I'll trade with you, Clara Lee."

"For real?" I asked.

"Sure," he said. "I'm starting to feel sick from the bouncing."

"Wow, thanks!"

I couldn't believe my Good Luck. It was happening already. My Good Luck day had officially begun.

During reading, Ms. Morgan picked me to read from our read-aloud book *The Witches*. We were at the part where the Grand High Witch turns Bruno into a mouse—also known as The Best Part of the Whole Book. I love to read aloud. Grandpa says I have the best reading voice he's ever heard.

And then, at lunch, Shayna had my favorite meatloaf and pickle sandwich and she let me have a bite. Max had gingersnaps and he gave me two broken ones. Max *never* shares his gingersnaps, not even with Georgina, and she's his twin sister.

All in all, it was a Great Luck lunch, and I had to wonder—how long was my luck gonna last? Would it be a Good Luck week? A Good Luck month? I personally hoped it would stay forever, but I doubted that Good Luck worked like that. I was sure Good Luck had other people to visit. The magic would have to fade at some point. But I figured it would at least last me the rest of the day. Wouldn't it?

When I went to P.E., I got my answer. We were doing the rope climb, and not once in my whole life have I ever been able to do the rope climb. I only get but so far and then I dangle like a gummy worm on a hook. It just isn't pretty and it's very embarrassing. And scary. So I stopped trying. What was the point when I knew I couldn't do it?

But it was my Good Luck day, so on that day, I knew I could. I just knew it. When Mr. Eddly asked for volunteers, I raised my hand high. I thought to myself, *Now that I have Luck on my side, it should be no problem.*

Mr. Eddly looked very surprised to see my hand in the air. "Really, Clara Lee? I thought you said climbing rope wasn't 'your style.'" When he said it he did that thing where he makes bunny ears with his fingers. He always does that when he wants to make a point.

I stood up and shrugged. "What was out of style yesterday could be back today, Mr. Eddly. You just never know." Then I walked past him with a little sashay in my step.

"Well good for you, Clara Lee," said Mr. Eddly. He looked impressed.

I walked right up to that rope without so much as a fear in my heart. Because if my grandpa said I had Good Luck, then I knew it was true.

I grabbed that rope and started to climb.

And climb, and climb. When I got scared, I didn't look down, I just kept climbing. Even when I got tired, I kept going. But then I got to that part of the rope where I usually jump off. For a minute there, I didn't know if I could keep on going. But then I said to myself, "Come on, Good Luck. Take it to the top."

And then I did it! I could hardly believe I was there on top, the first time in my whole life, with Shayna and Max and Georgina and Mr. Eddly all clapping for me. Max whistled loudly.

"Good job, Clara Lee," called up Mr. Eddly. "You can come down now."

I grinned and I gave a little wave. Everybody waved back. Then I thought to myself, *Whoa, this is pretty high up*, and I started to climb down. About halfway there, I thought, *What the heck, I'll jump off*. And then I said

something I heard in a movie once. "Yippy-ka-yay!" I yelled, and I jumped off.

I landed on the cushiony pad with a thud. I couldn't wait to get home and tell Grandpa all about it.

After, Shayna asked me, "How did you do that, Clara Lee? I thought you were afraid of the rope."

I scrunched up my lips to the side. "I never said I was afraid of the rope."

"Well, you said you didn't like being up so high," she said.

"That's not the same as being afraid."

"Sounds like the same thing to me," Shayna said stubbornly. "How'd you do it today?"

I looked at her for a minute. Shayna was my best friend. I could trust her. "It's because of my Good Luck," I said at last.

"Huh?"

"See, I had a dream where my grandpa died—"

Shayna clapped her hand over her mouth. "That's not Good Luck, that's terrible luck!" she said with a worried frown. Shayna really likes my grandpa.

"No, silly, in my Korean culture, when someone dies in a dream, that's Good Luck."

"That doesn't make any sense," she said. "I don't think I believe in luck anyway. *My* grandma says we make our own luck."

"Well is your grandma a world-renowned dream genius?" I challenged.

"No, I don't *think* so...."

"If she was, you'd know it. Trust me. My grandpa is, and he's training me to be one."

"I still don't believe it," Shayna said. But there was doubt in her eyes.

"Just wait and see," I told her, tapping her

on the nose the way Grandpa does sometimes. "All kinds of good stuff is gonna happen to me today."

Shayna swatted my hand away. "Yeah, we'll see."

I smiled. "Yes, you will."

CHAPTER 6

When we got our squirrel stories back in Language Arts, mine was an A-plus. I lifted it up and showed it to Shayna. I pointed at the paper and mouthed, *Good Luck*.

Shayna shrugged. "You always get A's on your stories," she whispered.

"But not an A-plus," I reminded her.

Shayna just shrugged again. "Can I borrow your eraser? Mine's all nubby."

Sighing, I reached inside my desk, and my fingers touched something definitely non-eraserlike. So I pulled it out, and would you believe, it was a candy necklace, wrapped in plastic!

Wowza. Where did that come from? It hadn't been there yesterday, that was for sure.

"Where'd you get that?" Shayna whispered.

I shook my head slowly. "I don't know...."

Shayna's eyes were bigger than the jumbo gumballs we get at the Chinese restaurant we go to sometimes. "Clara Lee, maybe you really *do* have Good Luck," she breathed, watching me rip the plastic wrapper off.

I put on the necklace and touched the candy pieces. Not even one piece was broken. Everybody knows that with a candy necklace, there's always at least one piece broken. Not this one. This one was perfect. I had a feeling it looked good on me. "I told you," I said, trying to catch a look at myself in Shayna's glasses.

"Keep me posted," she said, turning back to her math worksheet.

"I will."

"And give me your eraser, will you?"

I passed her my eraser, and instead of working on my math too, I started making a list. I love making lists. I wrote down:

And then I drew a little picture of me wearing a candy necklace. I did look pretty good in that necklace.

I was finishing up my list as Ms. Morgan was finishing up the afternoon announcements. "Our hardworking custodial staff asks that we only use as many paper towels as we need. It's easy to be green, kids."

She winked at us. "And the final announcement, for those of you who are interested in trying out for Little Miss Apple Pie, speeches are this Thursday during morning assembly. This year the theme is 'What makes our town so special?' You can sign up on the sign-up sheet hanging outside Mr. Charlevoix's music room."

Vince Peretti raised his hand. "Hey, Ms. Morgan, I wanna try out for Little Miss Apple Pie. Can I, oh please, can I?"

Everyone laughed, except Dionne Gregory and me. She turned around and said, "It's *not* funny. Little Miss Apple Pie is a Bramley tradition. You shouldn't make fun of it."

Dionne Gregory is a bit of a know-it-all type. She's always doing things like winning spelling bees and jump rope contests. She is just plain good at a lot of things. But for once, I kind of agreed with Dionne.

"Chill out, Dionne," Vince said, rolling his eyes. "I was just kidding."

Ms. Morgan said, "Vince, if you'd like to try out for Little Miss Apple Pie, you should talk to Mr. Charlevoix. He's on the committee."

"I *said* I was just kidding, Ms. Morgan," Vince said. "You couldn't pay me to try out for Little Miss Apple Pie."

I looked down at my list. What if I finally gave Little Miss Apple Pie a shot? With Good

Luck on my side, maybe I would be brave enough to give it a go. It could be just like the rope in P.E. Maybe Little Miss Apple Pie was the reason Good Luck even came to me to begin with. It was definitely something to think about.

I drew a teeny tiny little apple pie on my list. I didn't even dare write down the words "Little Miss Apple Pie." I didn't want to jinx it.

CHAPTER 7

On the bus ride home, Georgina compli-
mented me on my new necklace. She loves
jewelry. "Where'd you get that from?" she
asked.

I touched my necklace. "Um, I don't know," I

said. I wasn't ready to share the secret of my Good Luck just yet. For now, it was between me, Grandpa, and Shayna.

Max popped his head between Shayna and me. "Hey, that looks good on you, Clara Lee. Can I have a piece?"

"Um...no. Sorry," I said. Max's hands were always sticky, and the last thing I wanted was him getting any stickiness on my new necklace.

❀ ❀ ❀ ❀

When Emmeline and I walked home from the bus stop, she noticed my necklace right away. "Where'd you get that?" she demanded. "I want one!"

"It's a secret," I said with a secret little smile. Emmeline hates secrets worse than she hates tofu. Not me. I love secrets and I love tofu, especially the way Mom makes it. (She boils it and puts a little soy sauce and green onion on top. Delicious!)

Emmeline shouted, "You're not supposed to have secrets!"

"Says who?"

She didn't have an answer for that one right away. Then she brightened and gave me her best know-it-all look. "Says God!"

"God never said that," I told her. "And I should know, I've been going to Sunday school longer than you. I've been going to Sunday school since before you were even born."

She didn't have an answer for that one right away either. "Let me wear it to school tomorrow," she said at last. "Please? I'll give you the rest of my Raisinets."

"No way! I don't even like Raisinets and I

know for a fact that you don't either." It was just like Emmeline to try and give me her hand-me-down Raisinets.

"Please?"

"No. This candy necklace is going to be my signature look." I was already picturing myself wearing it at my birthday party, at my third grade graduation, maybe even at my wedding. And *posssssibly* on the Apple Blossom float.

"What's a signature look?" Emmeline wanted to know.

"It's a look that's signature. You know how when you sign something, it's called a signature? It's like how Grandpa uses a cane. That's his signature look," I explained. "Doesn't it look good on me?"

"Yeah," she said grudgingly.

I smiled at her. Maybe I would let her borrow it, in a couple of months, if I hadn't eaten it already....

"But not half as good as it's gonna look on me!" Emmeline said with an evil cackle. "Aha-hahaha!"

❁ ❁ ❁ ❁

As soon as we got home, I headed straight for the backyard. That's where the garden was, and that was where I would find Grandpa. The garden was his domain. He was the master of the land. My grandpa has the power to make things grow. He's like a magician.

In the fall, like now, we have squash and pumpkin and Dad makes pumpkin soup. Just like I knew he would be, Grandpa was out in the garden, stooped over, snatching up weeds like they were made of gold.

I ran up to him and yelled, "Hey!"

"Hay is for donkeys," Grandpa said.

I giggled. "Hay is for *horses*, Grandpa."

I gave him a hug. He smelled just like always, like grass and bread and those Vienna sausage links he loves to eat. I gave his sweater-vest a good sniff. It's the best smell in the world.

"Don't donkeys eat hay too?" he argued, grabbing another weed.

"Yeah, I guess so," I said, throwing my book bag on the grass and sitting on it.

"What happened at school today?" Grandpa asked me.

I reached into my pocket and pulled out my list. "*So much* happened. Listen," I said, and then I read him my list. "Backseat, sandwich, gingersnaps, read aloud *Witches*—part when Bruno turns into a mouse, rope, candy necklace."

"What that mean?" Grandpa wanted to know.

"It means that I had some Good Luck today! The best luck," I explained. "I got to sit in the back of the bus, I had a really good lunch, I got to read out loud in class—"

"You are really good reader," Grandpa agreed.

"*And* I climbed the rope in P.E.!"

Grandpa stopped weeding and said, "Isn't that rope dangerous?"

"No, it's safe, there are cushions and everything!" Then I lifted up my candy necklace. "Isn't it gorgeous?"

"What's gorgeous?"

"It means really, really, really pretty," I said.

"How you spell?" Grandpa dropped his weeds and pulled out his notebook and pen.

"Um, G-O-R—" I hesitated. How did you spell "gorgeous," anyway? "J-O-U-S."

Grandpa wrote it down and said, "You shore?"

"Uh-huh, definitely," I said.

Grandpa said, "Clara-yah, you are gor-jous."

I laughed. I felt really gor-jous too, with my candy necklace and everything. Maybe even gor-jous enough for Little Miss Apple Pie. "So guess what?"

"What?"

"I might try out for Little Miss Apple Pie this year." I watched closely for his reaction.

Grandpa's forehead wrinkled. "Little Miss Apple Pie?"

"Remember, at Apple Blossom Festival last year? She wears a red sash and she stands on the float and waves to everybody." I plopped down on the ground and waved up at him, princess-style. "I want to be her."

"Sounds good to me," said Grandpa. "You'd be real cute on that float. A natural."

I looked up at him. "You're just saying that 'cause you're my grandpa, Grandpa."

He shook his head. "No way. Grandpa never lies."

I guessed that was true. I'd never known Grandpa to lie. Maybe I *would* be a natural. Me in my red dress with my new candy necklace.

Emmeline didn't mention the necklace again for the rest of the day.

I thought she'd forgotten all about it, and I relaxed. Until dinner. Emmeline is good at the sneak attack. She is proof that you should never, ever underestimate your enemy.

"Mommy, Clara Lee won't share her necklace with me," she announced.

Mom looked up from her bowl of ramen. Ramen is what Daddy cooks when Mom's home late from her office. "That's a cute necklace, Clara," she said. "Where'd you get it?"

"Don't you love it? It was a gift," I said, twirling some ramen on my fork. I wished I could eat ramen with chopsticks the way Mom and Daddy and Grandpa did.

"Looks good on you," Grandpa said. Daddy said so too.

"Well, she won't share it," Emmeline whined. "I want to wear it *tomorrow*."

I waited for Mom to say, Now Clara, you should share. Mom is big on sharing. She's always saying how big sisters should share with little sisters, how sharing is caring.

But she didn't say that. She said, "Now Emmeline, Clara just got that necklace as a gift. I think you should let her have it to herself for a little while. Maybe next week Clara will let you borrow it."

Emmeline looked like she was gonna go into shock. The look on her face said, Huh? Mine did too.

"But...sharing is caring, Mommy. Remember?" She looked around the table for backup. Grandpa shrugged sympathetically.

Daddy said, "Sharing is definitely caring, Em. Now how about you share some of that kimchi with me?"

And that was the end of that. I had my candy

necklace all to myself, and for once in my life, I didn't have to share with Emmeline. Anytime soon, anyway. My luck was in full effect.

That night, I almost didn't want to go to bed. What if I had a Bad Luck dream that scared Good Luck away? What if Bad Luck came to hang out with me instead? I could forget all about Little Miss Apple Pie, that was for sure.

I didn't dream about anything that night, at least not that I remembered. And a dream just doesn't count unless you remember it.

CHAPTER 8

I woke up extra early the next morning, and the first thing I thought was, *Is Good Luck still here?* I said it out loud too, just to make it feel more real. "Good Luck, are you still here?"

Emmeline swung her head down from her top bunk and said, "Huh?"

"Never you mind," I told her.

She shrugged and swung her head back up top. "Gonna sleep for five more minutes so you better keep quiet, Clara Lee," she said.

"Bah humbug," I said, in a voice that was the opposite of quiet.

Then I said, "I think I smell pancakes."

Emmeline said, "Pancakes?" Now she was as wide awake as I was. She was right behind me when I went downstairs to investigate. I couldn't wait one more minute to find out all the great things that were gonna happen.

Mom had made banana pancakes for breakfast. "Get it while it's hot, girls," she said, pouring syrup on our pancakes.

Emmeline and I ran to our seats. Usually

we have cereal. We only ever eat pancakes on Saturdays and snow days.

"Mom, can I have extra?" I asked, taking my first bite.

Mom nodded and poured a little more.

"Me too," said Emmeline, the little copycat.

After I ate, Grandpa braided my hair in two perfect braids, and he didn't even have to do a do-over. Daddy let me watch five extra minutes of cartoons before he dropped us off at the bus stop on his way to work. Usually, we walk to the bus stop, but like I said, it was a special day already. There was nothing *usual* about it.

Even Emmeline was on her best behavior. She let me have the last banana pancake, and she didn't complain when I drank all the orange juice. She even let me sit up front with Daddy instead of complaining like she always does.

It was official. Luck was still here. My mind was made up. I was trying out for Little Miss Apple Pie.

When I got to Ms. Morgan's classroom, Shayna was already sitting in her seat. She was wearing a yellow sweater and a yellow headband. Shayna loves matching. "Shayna, I have to tell you something," I said, sliding into my seat.

Dionne Gregory was in her seat two desks away, and she looked over at us. She is always in everybody's business.

I lowered my voice. "I'm gonna try out for Little Miss Apple Pie."

Shayna's brown eyes turned big. "For real? I thought you were too scared to make a speech in front of everybody."

"I never said I was *scared*. I just said I didn't want to do it. But now I do. Now that I've got Good Luck, I might really have a chance. What do you think?"

"I think you have to go for it." Shayna held up her hand and we high-fived.

Then I reached inside for my favorite pencil, and instead I found a gingersnap. The very same kind of gingersnap that Max always brought for lunch. Why would he put a ginger-snap in my desk?

I decided to write him a note and find out. I wrote, "Max, did you put this gingersnap in my desk?" Then I drew three little boxes for yes, no, and maybe. I passed it to Shayna and whis-pered, "Pass it on to Max."

I could tell Shayna didn't want to because Shayna doesn't like passing notes, but she did it anyway. She passed it to Natalie, who passed it to Vince, who pretended like he was gonna open it, but then he passed it to Max. Max opened it up and read it. Then he checked one of the boxes and passed it to Simon, who passed it to Evie, who passed it to Shayna, who passed it to me.

He checked no. Huh? If Max didn't put the gingersnap in my desk, who did? Good Luck?

"Was it you, Good Luck?" I whispered.

Shayna poked me on the arm and said, "Are you talking to yourself, Clara Lee?"

"No," I said quickly.

"It sounded like you were."

"I wasn't, I wasn't. Hey, I think Ms. Morgan's coming back," I said, pointing at the door.

That hushed Shayna up right away. Shayna is always worried about getting into trouble.

I took a bite of my cookie and leaned back in my seat. "Thanks for the cookie, Good Luck," I whispered with a mouthful of gingersnap.

Shayna turned to me and said, "Huh?" but I pointed at Ms. Morgan and she turned back around, so quick one of her braids whipped me!

"Ow," I whispered in a loud voice—even though, truth be told, it didn't really hurt.

When it was time for music, I didn't go inside the music room right away. I went straight over to the sign-up sheet hanging outside Mr. Charlevoix's door. The only name on it so far was Dionne's, in oh-so-perfect cursive. I made a face at it. Then I signed my name right below, only my cursive didn't look as good as hers, not nearly. I messed up my capital *L*. I thought about scratching it out and trying again, but decided that would look even worse, so I left it the way it was.

❀ ❀ ❀ ❀

Dionne came up to me during recess. Shayna, Georgina, and I were jumping rope.

"I saw your name on the sign-up sheet, Clara Lee," she said.

I kept jumping. "Yup."

"I think it's great you're trying out."

"Thanks," I said.

"I'm trying out too. Did you know that my great-great-great-uncle was one of Bramley's founding fathers?"

"No," I said. I stopped jumping.

"My mom thinks I should automatically be Little Miss Apple Pie just for that." Dionne

rolled her eyes, like, Isn't my mom so crazy? "Since my family partly founded this town and all."

"Neat," I said sourly. "Maybe you'll get it, then."

"I hope so. I mean, I hope you get it too." She paused. "Did I tell you my mom was Little Miss Apple Pie when she was in elementary school? My grandma too. It sort of runs in our family. You know, 'cause we're as American as apple pie. We're probably the oldest family in Bramley. When did your family come to Bramley, Clara Lee?"

"I'm not sure," I said. I could feel a little lump rising in my throat.

Then Shayna came up next to us and put her arm around me. "Dionne, we're going to jump rope now."

"Sure," Dionne said. "Good luck, Clara Lee."

When she was gone, Shayna said, "Don't you listen to her, Clara Lee."

Georgina said, "Dionne Gregory thinks she knows it all but she doesn't know anything about anything."

Shayna and Georgina started swinging the jump rope, and I jumped in. But my heart wasn't in it. Wasn't my family as American as apple pie too? Grandpa came from Korea, but both my mom and dad were born in America, just like me. I deserved to have a shot at Little Miss Apple Pie as much as Dionne did. Didn't I?

❀ ❀ ❀ ❀

When I got on the bus that afternoon, I sat on the window side, even though I like the aisle better because I can talk to more people that way. I was too depressed to talk to people. I felt about as low as a flea on a dead dog. How could I compete with the founder of this town's great-great-great-niece?

Shayna patted my shoulder and tried to cheer me up, but I just wasn't feeling it. All I wanted to do was stare out the window.

Then Max said, "Hey, Shayna, will you switch seats with me?"

Shayna looked at me and shrugged. "Sure," she said.

She got up and Max sat down. He fished around in his backpack and handed me a gingersnap, which of course I snatched right up. I might have been depressed, but I wasn't too depressed for a gingersnap.

"Thanks," I said, stuffing it into my mouth. Wait a minute. I thought Max didn't have any gingersnaps today....

"You're welcome," he said. Then he looked over his shoulder and around the bus before he asked in a quiet voice, "Clara Lee, will you be my valentine?"

My mouth was still full, and I said, "Huh? It's not even Valentine's Day."

"I know that," he said very seriously. "I want you to be my valentine all the days of the year, not just on Valentine's Day."

"Um," I said. "Did you put that cookie in my desk?"

"Of course. I put that necklace in there too," he said, pointing at my neck.

I was starting to wish I hadn't taken his necklace, or his gingersnap. I didn't want to be anybody's valentine and I definitely didn't want to be Max's. Max was my buddy and that was it. I said, "But... I thought that came from someplace else."

"Where else would it come from?"

"I thought it came from my Good Luck," I said.

"Good Luck?" Max repeated. "That doesn't make any scientific sense, Clara Lee. There's no such thing as good or bad luck."

I stared at him. "Yes, there is."

"Look, do you want to be my valentine or not?"

"No," I said meanly. "I don't want to be your valentine at all."

Max looked mad. He said, "Then give me back my necklace!"

"No! You gave it to me as a *gift*! You can't take it back!"

Max reached over and tried to grab it off my neck, and I held on with all my might. "Give it!"

"It's mine!"

"Give it!"

And that's when the string holding the necklace together snapped. And the candy pieces fell all over my lap and the seat. My precious necklace. My signature look.

"Now look what you've done!" I yelled. I could feel tears prickling the backs of my eyes like needles.

Max looked sorry, but not that sorry. "It was my necklace anyway," he said, picking up a few pieces and popping one in his mouth.

"Look, Max, when you give something to someone, it's not yours anymore. Get it?" Then I took my foot and kicked him off the seat, kinda sorta hard. Max landed on the ground with a thud. He had tears in his eyes. Whoops. Maybe I had gone too far.

"I don't want you to be my valentine anymore, Clara Lee," Max said, getting up and

wiping away tears with the back of his hand. "You're just a big show-off, and your hair isn't that pretty anyway. And you know what? I hope you don't win Little Miss Apple Pie either because you don't deserve it!"

Then he grabbed his backpack and moved up two seats.

Shayna tapped me on the shoulder and said, "Hey, what's going on?"

"Why'd you push my brother?" Georgina asked me with accusing eyes.

"None of your business," I said, turning back around.

"Clara Lee!" Shayna said. But I wouldn't turn back around. I was afraid I might cry, and there was nothing I hated worse than crying in front of people.

CHAPTER 9

What's the matter, Clara Lee?" Emmeline asked me on the walk home from the bus stop.

"Nothing," I told her.

"Uh-huh, there's something," she insisted. "I can tell. Sister to sister, what's wrong?"

I sighed. Pushing a rock along the ground with my toe, I said, "Remember how I had that Good Luck dream?"

"Uh-huh."

"Well, I had Good Luck for a while and now it's gone and all I've got left is Bad Luck." I let out a big gust of air. "Dionne Gregory doesn't think I'm American as apple pie enough to be Little Miss Apple Pie."

"Dionne Gregory is a baha bighead."

"What's a baha bighead?"

"It's someone who thinks they know it all," Emmeline explained. "Kinda like how you're a baha bighead sometimes."

I frowned at her.

"But not today," she added quickly.

"Thanks," I said. "And that's not all. Me and

88

Max had a fight and I kicked him out of the seat and now everybody hates me."

"You shouldn't have kicked him out of the seat," Emmeline said with a shrug. "Duh."

"I know that!"

"Then why'd you do it?"

"I don't know," I said miserably. "I guess I was just mad about that stuff with Dionne."

"He's probably gonna tell on you when he gets home and you're gonna get in trouble with Mom and Daddy and Grandpa. I bet his mom is gonna call. You want me to distract them when the phone rings?"

"That's okay, Max wouldn't tell," I said. I mean, I doubted he'd tell. He was no tattletale. It wasn't his style. But he did look pretty mad sitting there on the ground. Maybe he would tell.

When we got home, I took off my shoes like always and was about to sneak off to my room so I wouldn't have to tell Grandpa about every-thing that happened that day. Grandpa was in the TV room watching one of his Korean soap operas, the kind where the women are always crying and the men wear fancy suits.

He had his back to me and I was sneaking past him when he said, "Welcome home! Come give Grandpa a hug."

I swear, my grandpa has eyes in the back of his head.

I went over and gave him a hug, but it was a limp green bean kind of hug. My heart wasn't in it.

"What's wrong with my Clara?" He patted the cushion next to him.

I plopped down on the couch. I didn't want to make him feel bad for our family not being American as apple pie enough, but I'd never lied to him before either. Grandpa and I don't lie to each other.

I let out a big sigh. "Well, remember that Little Miss Apple Pie thing I told you about?"

Grandpa nodded.

"I don't think I'm gonna try out anymore," I said. My voice came out sounding so little and shaky, it made me feel even sadder. I could not look at him. If I saw Grandpa looking at me with sorry eyes, I just knew I would cry and maybe never stop.

"Why you not try out?" he wanted to know.

"Because Dionne Gregory was saying how her great-great-great-uncle was one of the founders of this town, and how her family is all-American. American as apple pie." I sniffled.

"What's this, American as apple pie?"

"It just means really, really American," I said.

"So what? So are you, American as apple pie."

"I don't think I'm as American as Dionne Gregory," I said, wiping a tear away.

"Clara-yah, of course you are! You are all-American Korean American!" Grandpa put his arm around me. "You are both. One hundred percent American, one hundred percent Korean. Doesn't make you less than anybody else. It makes you more."

"I don't know," I said.

"*I* know. Trust Grandpa. I am telling you the truth. You trust Grandpa?"

I nodded.

"Good. You remember that and be proud, Clara-yah."

I snuggled in close to Grandpa and said, "So you think I should still try out?"

"Of course I do." He took his handkerchief out of his pocket and wiped my teary face.

"So maybe I will," I said.

"That's my Clara!" Grandpa lifted his hand for a high five, which of course, yours truly taught him. We high-fived so hard my hand stung. What did Dionne know about it anyway? Georgina was right. Dionne Gregory didn't know nothin' 'bout nothin'.

But there was still one more thing. "Grandpa,

there's one more thing. I'm in a fight with Max and everybody's mad at me."

"What happened? Max is nice boy."

I hesitated. "Well, Max wanted me to be his valentine."

"What you mean, valentine?"

"Max wanted me to be his girlfriend," I explained.

"Girlfriend? You are too young to be some-body's girlfriend. You gotta be free," Grandpa said, shaking his head. "You told him no thank you?"

"Not exactly. I told him no, and he said he wanted his necklace back, but I didn't want to give it to him. So I kicked him out of the seat and he fell down." I said the last part very quickly because I was hoping Grandpa wouldn't understand me.

But he did. He shook his head again and said, "Ah. That's not nice."

"I know," I whispered. I felt like the crummiest crumb of a friend ever.

"When boy likes you, you say no thank you. You don't kick him on the ground."

"I know," I said. "Even if he *did* break my necklace."

Grandpa gave me a stern look, so I added, "But you're right, Grandpa. I still shouldn't have kicked him. I know that now."

"What you gonna do now?"

"Say sorry?"

"Good girl."

I felt better already. Grandpa always knows the right thing to say.

At bath time that night, Mom said, "How about we make it a bubble bath tonight, buddy?"

I figured Grandpa must have told her about our talk. I also figured I could use a bubble bath.

I sat on the toilet lid with my favorite brown bear towel wrapped tight around my shoulders like a superhero cape while Mom got the water running, making sure it was hot and bubbly enough. She tested the water and poured in some more bubble bath. "So, have you given some thought to your big speech?" she asked casually.

"A little," I said.

"Just think about what you love most about Bramley," she suggested.

"What do *you* love most about Bramley?"

Mom turned the faucet off and sat on the

edge of the tub. She blew her hair out of her face and thought it over. "Hmm. Let's see. Well, I love that Bramley is safe for my two girls. I love that you can play out in the yard all day and I don't have to worry. I love that we can drive to the ocean, or the mountains, or the city and then come back home to Bramley. I love the people too. We have great neighbors."

Mom got up and wiped her bubbly hands on her jeans. "Get in that tub and start thinking, girl." She kissed me on the top of my head and left me alone with my thoughts.

I got in the tub and started thinking about what makes Bramley so special. I guess everybody thinks their town is something special, but *I* think our town is something *super* special.

I've lived in Bramley my whole life, so I don't have anywhere else to compare it to. But it's not like you have to compare chocolate-caramel-marshmallow-brownie ice cream to something else to know that what you've got is pretty great.

As I played with my rubber frog, I thought about the town barber shop, which doesn't have a name, just a sign that says BARBER SHOP. My grandpa and I go there together. It's our special thing, no Emmeline. She came once and couldn't sit still and now she doesn't want to go back. Which is her loss. Grandpa always buys me an Eskimo pie at the market next door and then I sit and watch him get his hair cut. It doesn't take that long; he doesn't have a lot of hair. What he does have is gray and soft and like a kitten tail. Mine is long and black as night and we do it all different kinds of ways. Sometimes two braids, sometimes one, sometimes two ponytails, sometimes one. I have the longest hair in my family.

My mom's is above her shoulders and Emmeline's is like a little bowl around her head.

Only Grandpa and Daddy get their hair cut at the barber shop though. Us ladies go to Colette's in the middle of town. It is pink, pink, pink. Daddy says it looks like someone upchucked Pepto-Bismol at Colette's, but I think it's beautiful. Just like Miss Colette herself. By the way, Colette is not her real name, it is Colleen. But she says Colette sounds fancier and Frencher and I agree.

Not only that, our town has Cooper's Drugstore. At Cooper's Drugstore, you can sit at the counter and order a tuna fish sandwich and an ice-cream soda, and Mr. Cooper will take out his glass eye and let you look at it. There's also Sweetie Pie Bakery next door, with the prettiest cakes around.

We also have a bookstore called Books &

Books & Books, where there is a whole separate kids' area with beanbags and you can sit and read for as long as your mom will let you. They have maybe a million books, and I plan on reading them all before high school. I think I've read about two hundred and fifty-one, so I have a ways to go but I'm getting close.

Our library is nice too. The librarians Mrs. Shelby and Mr. Kleinfeld help you with whatever you need help on. They never shush.

The more I thought about it, the more I was sure. Our town really was special. I doubted other towns had a Mr. Cooper or a Miss Colette. I stayed in the bathtub thinking about this stuff for so long that my fingers turned pruney and Emmeline banged on the door saying she had to go.

"Use Mommy and Daddy's bathroom," I yelled back. "I'm thinking in here."

When I finally got out of the tub and dried off, I wrote down all the stuff I'd been thinking about.

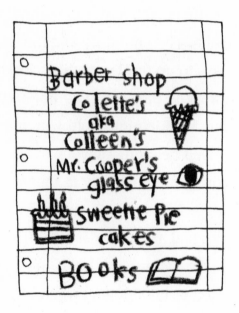

CHAPTER 10

On the bus that next morning, I tried to catch Max's eye, but he would not look at me. Georgina was giving me the silent treatment too. The only person who would give me the time of day was Shayna. I was glad I had her as a best friend.

When you want the day to go by quick, it goes as slow as a ketchup drip. When you want it to go by slow, it's like somebody hit the Heinz right on the 57 and it happens all at once. Ketchup, ketchup everywhere.

It was like that with the assembly. I wanted the day to drip by slowly but the assembly came up so fast.

Dionne and I were the only girls from the third grade trying out to be Little Miss Apple Pie. The other girls were in fourth and fifth, and they went first, oldest to youngest. A fifth grader mentioned how almost everyone in Bramley recycled, and how we were a very green town. One fourth grader talked about how Bramley was special for its delicious apples and how everyone in America wished they had apples as good as ours.

I took a quick peek around the auditorium, and my heart started to beat triple, quadruple time. The whole school was here.

Dionne went up before me. She was wearing a red dress and white tights with little red hearts. It looked like a new outfit. She already looked like Little Miss Apple Pie. I wished I was wearing red too.

"Bramley," she began, "is a town with great tradition."

Then she went on about how her great-great-great-uncle was a founding father, how her mother was Little Miss Apple Pie a long time ago, and how she, Dionne, was keeping tradition alive.

Her speech sounded really good. She told

a lot of facts about Bramley, and I wished I'd thought of that. I could tell she'd practiced a lot. She paused and smiled in all the right places.

When Dionne finished, everyone clapped. Then Mr. Charlevoix went to the microphone and said, "Next we have Clara Lee."

I felt like I was gonna barf all over Georgina, who was in the seat in front of me. Shayna grabbed my hand and gave it a squeeze. "Good *luck*," she whispered.

She gave me a knowing nod, and I gulped

and nodded back at her. As I walked up to the stage, I tried to walk tall, the way Grandpa told me.

When I got to the platform, I took a deep breath and looked out into the crowd. Everyone stared back at me. Shayna mouthed *good luck* again. I saw Emmeline with the first graders, and she waved, so I waved back.

I licked my lips. I'd practiced this on the bus. I could do this. "Bramley is special to me because of the people and the places." I took another deep breath. "We have a library where

the librarians Mrs. Shelby and Mr. Kleinfeld don't shush at you. They help you find whatever book you need. We have a bookstore where you can sit all day and read. We have Barber Shop, where the haircuts are fast and cheap, and we have Colette's, which is the pinkest place I've ever been in. And we have Sweetie Pie Bakery, where they always give you a free rainbow cookie if you tell them their cakes are pretty. Which they are. We have Cooper's Drugstore, where Mr. Cooper will make you an ice-cream soda and then show you his fake eyeball."

Some of the kids laughed; some teachers too. It made me feel braver. "That is what makes Bramley so special. The people. And that includes me and you."

I turned around and pointed at Mr. Charlevoix. "Mr. Charlevoix, you too. And Ms. Morgan.

And my sister, Emmeline. And my friends Shayna and Georgina and Max. We are all special. Thank you."

Everyone clapped. Then I gave a little bow, and I walked back to my seat with some swagger and just a touch of attitude. *Star* attitude. Getting up in front of people wasn't so bad. In fact, it was kind of fun.

I sat down and looked over at Max. He was looking back at me. *I'm sorry*, I mouthed.

He shrugged. He still looked a little mad.

I'm really *sorry*, I mouthed.

He shrugged again. And then he mouthed back, *It's okay.*

I breathed a big sigh of relief. We were friends again.

CHAPTER 11

Let's take a vote," I said on the bus that afternoon. "Who do you guys think is gonna win?"

Georgina said, "Dionne was really good...
but so were you, Clara Lee." Georgina is a very
loyal person.

"I vote you too, Clara Lee," Max said. He smiled at me. It felt nice to be forgiven.

"Thanks guys," I said. "Shayna, what do *you* think?"

"I think you guys were both really good, and so was that fifth grader who talked about the environment," said Shayna.

Well, that was good enough for Georgina and Max, 'cause they went right back to talking about Georgina's new kitten, Pony. Georgina named him Pony because a pony was what she really wanted and a kitten is what she got. Max wanted to train Pony to hiss at people, and Georgina wanted to enter Pony into a kitten modeling contest she heard about on the Internet. But I didn't care about Pony at that moment, because *I* really needed to know what Shayna's true thoughts were.

I whispered to Shayna, "Best friend to best friend, do you think I'm gonna win?"

Shayna whispered back, "Yes. You really were good, and plus, you're the only one with the good luck, remember?"

"I don't know," I said. "I think my Good Luck might have gone away. Yesterday I had that fight with Max. That doesn't sound like Good Luck to me at all."

"But maybe Good Luck will come back," Shayna said.

I thought that over. I mean, it was possible. Maybe it *would* come back to me! I was pretty sure Dionne hadn't had a special Good Luck death dream this week. It wasn't like she had a special Korean dream genius for a grandfather. That I knew of, anyway.

CHAPTER 12

For dinner that night, we had my not-so-favorite fish soup. Well, everyone except Emmeline. That picky eater Emmeline got hot wings. She got hot wings while the rest of us ate Mom's fish soup. Grandpa says Emmeline is a true dragon because that is the year she was born and because she only likes spicy foods: kimchi and hot wings. I don't know why she gets to be a dragon and I have to be a cow.

As soon as I saw that soup on the stove, I got worried. Did my Good Luck really up and leave? Did it decide to go be with someone else? Someone like Dionne Gregory? Good Luck couldn't really be gone, not when I needed it most.

When we sat down to eat, I could tell everybody was very tired and not in the cheeriest of moods. Daddy came home from work late, and he forgot to pick up the dry cleaning, which Mom muttered about.

I took a bite of fish soup and watched Emmeline chew on a hot wing, and I thought, *Now is the perfect time to cheer everybody up and tell them about Little Miss Apple Pie.* I couldn't hold in my big news a second longer. I was a stuffed piñata ready to pop! And even though I hadn't technically won or anything, I figured I might as well announce it.

"Guess what, everybody? I tried out for Little Miss Apple Pie today. I gave a speech about how special Bramley is. I think it was pretty good," I added, trying not to sound too braggy.

"Really, Clara? That's wonderful, buddy," Mom said, putting another hot wing on Emmeline's plate.

Grandpa beamed at me and said, "I'm so proud of my brave Clara."

"Well, I didn't win yet, guys," I said. I was so happy I ate a big bite of fish soup and rice. "But if I do win, I'll be on the float on Saturday."

"Your speech was good, Clara Lee," Emmeline said. Then she said, "In music, Mr. C told me I sing like a bird."

I gave her a dirty look. It was just like her to try and steal my shine.

"Mr. C said I was a star," she went on. Mr. C was what all the little kids called Mr. Charlevoix because they didn't know how to pronounce it the French way—Shar-luh-vwah.

"He said you were a star?" I repeated.

First graders were too little to sing. They were just babies! They were practically kinder-garteners! They didn't have any business onstage. What did they know about star quality?

"Uh-huh," she said, gnawing on a wing. "We sang 'Rockin' Robber.'"

"It's not 'Rockin' Robber,' it's 'Rockin' *Robin*,'" I told her, shaking my head.

"Nuh-uh," Emmeline said.

"Yuh-huh," I said, snatching one of the hot wings off Emmeline's plate.

She glared at me. "You better give me back my wing, Clara."

I bit into her wing. It was hot and juicy. "Sharing is caring, remember? Isn't that right, Mom?"

Before Mom could answer, Daddy said, "Clara, sharing is not the same thing as taking without asking. Taking without asking is called stealing." He took a bite of soup and looked at Emmeline's hot wings like he wanted to take one too. "Emmeline, how would you like to share one of those hot wings with Daddy?"

"No thank you," said Emmeline. "Now please make that thief give me back my hot wing!"

"I'm no thief," I told Daddy. "I just thought my own sister wouldn't mind sharing her wing with me."

"Give me back my wing, you thief!" Emmeline yelled. Her face was starting to get red like she might cry.

What a baby. What an absolute crybaby.

"Em, don't yell," said Mom, rubbing her forehead like she had a headache. "Clara, if you want wings, I'll heat up a couple for you, but don't go taking your sister's. Now give her back her wing."

"But I already bit into it," I said. "See?" I held up the wing for everybody to see.

"I WANT MY WING!" Emmeline screamed. She reached over and pinched my arm, my wing-eating arm.

Ooh, that really burned me up inside. I was so mad I couldn't help it—I threw the wing at Emmeline and it bounced off her head and onto her plate.

"CLARA LEE!" Mom yelled.

"Uhmma, I thought you said no yelling," I said, looking at her with big, confused eyes. I call her Uhmma when I know I'm about to get it. And by it, I mean *trouble*.

Then Grandpa said, "Clara-yah, you are very bad girl tonight." The corners of his mouth turned down and he looked like a sad old man. More than anything else, he looked tired. Like maybe he wished he lived in his own house.

My eyes filled with tears. I hated to be the one who made Grandpa's mouth turn down like that. Why couldn't Emmeline have been the one to make him look sad and tired? Why me? It was all her fault; she was the one who interrupted my story about Little Miss Apple Pie.

"You can finish your dinner in your room if you keep at it," Daddy said.

"I don't want to finish my dinner in my room," I said. "I barely even like fish soup."

Mom said, "Kid, you're stretching my patience here. Don't press your luck."

Yikes. No more buddy. I was kid now. No use pressing my luck. I shut my mouth and took a bite of fish soup to show how sorry I was.

Then Emmeline licked hot sauce off her fingers and grinned a toothy grin at me. She looked like a scary jack-o'-lantern with her missing front tooth. "Rockin' robber, tweet, tweet, tweetly-tweet," she sang.

I stood up. That was it. I'd had it. "It's 'Rockin' ROBIN'!" I yelled.

"UPSTAIRS!" Mom and Daddy yelled.

I glared at them. "Just so you know, you're both yelling now too." And because I was still hungry, and *not* because I liked it, I grabbed my bowl of fish soup. "And I'll be taking *this* with me!"

Then I scooted off before I could get into any more trouble.

It was very clear that Good Luck had left the building. It was also very clear that I could forget about Little Miss Apple Pie. So much for my crowd-pleasing speech.

CHAPTER 13

I didn't speak one word to Emmeline all night. I was giving her the silent treatment. But she didn't even notice.

When we were brushing our teeth, I decided to end the silent treatment. I hissed at her,

"Because of you, I had to eat alone in my room!"

I hissed because I didn't want to get in trouble with Mom and Daddy and Grandpa again. But my mouth was full of toothpaste when I hissed it, and Emmeline said, "Huh? You sound like a snake, Clara Lee. Talk right."

So I spat out the toothpaste and hissed it

again. "Because of you, I had to eat alone in my room!"

"So-rry," she said, not looking one bit sorry. "But you shouldn't have taken my wing."

"I'll take what I want," I grumped, stomping

back to *my* bedroom. Well, it used to be my bedroom. Now it was our bedroom.

I was tempted to lock the door on Emmeline, but the last thing I needed was another sad face from Grandpa. So instead I put on my pink polka-dot pajama dress and climbed into bed. But even my pink polka-dot pajama dress didn't cheer me up. I was un-cheer-up-able.

I crossed my arms and stared up at the top bunk. It was over. Good Luck had left me in the dust. I was all alone now. It was just me, Clara Lee.

I made a list in my head. It was called "Bad Things That Happened to Me Today."

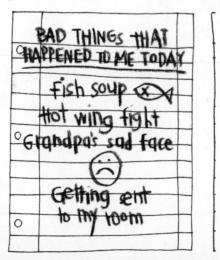

But the thing was, when I really thought about it, it wasn't an altogether bad day. Some good stuff happened too. I couldn't just forget about the good stuff. So then I made a list that was called "Good Things That Happened to Me Today."

I figured the speech and friendship counted for more than fish soup and a hot wing fight.

Maybe the good and the bad balanced each other out. Maybe there was no such thing as good or bad luck days. Maybe every day had good and bad things, and that was just the way it went.

CHAPTER 14

That night, I slept and at first nothing happened. But then…I dreamed the Good Luck dream! It happened all over again, but it was a little bit different this time. There was Grandpa and me, walking to the barber shop. There was the Mustache Man, coming up behind us in a chariot, and then he threw an apple at Grandpa's head and then Grandpa fell right over. Just like before.

When I woke up, my heart was beating so crazy, it felt like there was a pony prancing around in my chest. I almost leaped out of bed to check on Grandpa. And then I remembered. Grandpa wasn't even the tiniest bit dead. He was only dream-dead. Besides, I didn't think anybody could die in real life from being hit in the head by an apple.

Maybe it was just a dream. What if Max was right, and there was no such thing as good or bad luck?

But maybe not. Maybe it was a sign. And maybe, just maybe, Good Luck existed after all.

✿ ✿ ✿ ✿

All morning, I couldn't stop tapping my fingers and feet.

My teacher Ms. Morgan said, "Clara Lee, what's got you so worked up today?"

I smiled at her and shrugged mysteriously. She'd know why soon enough.

Ms. Morgan smiled at me and went back to writing on the chalkboard.

Then I turned to Shayna and whispered, "I can't wait for the big announcement!" I felt like a happy red balloon floating high in the sky.

She nodded quickly and looked back at the chalkboard.

"I really think I could win," I continued. "So far it's been my perfect Lucky day. Just look how good my braids are today—"

"Clara Lee! Shh!" Shayna whispered back. "I don't want to get in trouble!"

I felt like Shayna had pricked me in my stomach with a needle. Suddenly I was a droopy red balloon with the air all sucked out. I didn't always get Shayna in trouble, did I?

"Sorry," I whispered.

She ignored me and copied what Ms. Morgan was writing on the chalkboard. I sighed and started copying too. I didn't know if I could wait a whole day to find out if I was going to be on the float or not. But I guessed I'd have to.

❀ ❀ ❀

The day crawled by slower than a caterpillar up a tree. It was the exact opposite of the day before. Reading, lunch, P.E., music, social studies. And then, at last, it was finally, finally time for afternoon assembly in the auditorium.

As we waited for Mr. Charlevoix to make the big announcement, Shayna said, "Good luck, Clara Lee."

That is why Shayna is my best friend. Because she knows how to forgive.

"Thank you, Shayna," I said.

Then we hooked pinkies and waited. Dionne was sitting in the row in front of us, and she turned around. "Good luck, Clara Lee."

She gave me a sympathetic smile, like she'd already won. Maybe she already had. Since her family was so important, her mom was probably on the Apple Blossom committee. Maybe Dionne had inside info. She said, "I wish both of us could win. But if everybody got picked to be on the float, then who would be in the audience, right?"

"That's true," I said sourly. "Your speech was really good."

"Thanks," she said. She said thanks like she was used to saying it all the time, like she was used to hearing how great she was.

"Weren't you nervous getting up in front of everybody?" I asked her. "I sure was."

Dionne shook her head, and her curls bounced around. "Not really. I sing in my church choir all the time. I'm used to the spotlight. I was named after a famous singer. Celine Dion? Have you ever heard of her?"

"No," I said.

"Well, my mother loves her and so do I. My mother says I have a voice like an angel and it brings people joy when I get up onstage and sing. So I try to do it whenever I can."

When she turned back around, I wanted to yank the red ribbon out of her hair, but I didn't. Shayna gave my pinky a squeeze, which made me feel better.

Mr. Charlevoix went up to the stage. He was holding the red sash and the apple tiara. He set them down on the podium and then he straightened his tie and cleared his throat. "Ahem. I think we all learned a little something about what makes our town so *très* special yesterday. Everyone did a *magnifique* job with the Apple Blossom Festival speeches. But there can only be one Little Miss Apple Pie. It is an honor indeed."

Mr. Charlevoix always used such fancy

words. I wished he'd just get down to business and tell us who was gonna be on that float tomorrow.

"Without further ado..."

I held my breath, and Shayna and I tightened pinkies.

"This year's Little Miss Apple Pie is third grader Clara Lee!"

I couldn't believe it. I really couldn't. I felt like I might faint. Dionne looked like she was going to faint too. Shayna grabbed my arm and said, "Clara Lee, you did it!"

"Come on up, Clara Lee," Mr. Charlevoix called out.

I hugged Shayna and then I walked up to the stage. Mr. Charlevoix put the sash on me and he placed the crown on my head. "Congratulations," he said. "We'll all look out for you on the float tomorrow."

Mr. Charlevoix patted me on the back so I would go back to my seat.

But I didn't go back to my seat. Instead, I went up to the podium. Into the microphone, I said, "Thank you for honoring me with this award, Mr. Charlevoix and teachers of Bramley Elementary School. Thank you most of all to my grandpa, who is at home right now, and to my best friend Shayna Wilkerson. I couldn't have won this without her help."

Shayna waved at me from her seat, and I waved back. Then I saw Dionne, and her mouth was in the shape of an *O*. I felt a teeny bit bad for her, even after all the mean stuff she said to me the other day. So I went ahead and gave her a friendly little wave too. She waved back. She looked sour about it, but at least she waved.

"You can go sit down now, Clara Lee," said Mr. Charlevoix, smiling at me.

I bowed. I felt like the luckiest girl in the whole world. I felt like a candle on top of a birthday cake, burning oh-so-bright. Right then and there, I decided that from then on, I was making my own luck.

CHAPTER 15

On the morning of Apple Blossom Festival, I woke up extra early. I got my red dress out of the closet and I tried to put it on, but it was a lot more complicated than I remembered. I got my arms in the jacket sleeves, but I couldn't figure out how to tie the bow.

So I crept over to Mom and Daddy's room and knocked on the door.

"Mom! I need your help," I whispered loudly.

I kept on knocking until Mom came out. Her eyes were only halfway open, but even with halfway open eyes, she figured out my dress and got me looking good.

"Pretty girl," she said.

"Thanks, Mom," I said, and then I ran downstairs to the kitchen. I toasted myself an English muffin and poured myself an extra-tall glass of milk. I was going to need it today.

When Daddy came downstairs in his jogging clothes, he said, "Check out Little Miss Apple Pie! You look great, Clara."

"Thanks, Daddy." I was eating a piece of

peanut butter toast, my specialty. "Daddy, you're not gonna wear that, are you?"

Daddy looked down at his T-shirt he got for free from the bank. "You don't like my outfit?" He made a sad face, but I knew he was just fooling.

"Just making sure," I said. "I want everybody to look good."

Grandpa came downstairs then, wearing a red sweater-vest and a turtleneck and his good jeans. He clapped his hands when he saw me. "Clara-yah, you look like beautiful!"

"So do you, Grandpa," I said. "Daddy, look at what Grandpa's wearing."

Grandpa smiled and said to my dad, "You gonna change, right?"

Daddy threw his hands up in the air and said, "I'm just going for a quick run! I'll change when I get back, I promise."

"You better hurry, Daddy. I've got to be on that float by 9 AM."

"Okay, okay, I'm going." Daddy gave me a kiss on the cheek, stole a bite of my peanut butter toast, and went out the back door.

"Now, down to business," Grandpa said. "How we gonna do your hair?"

"I'm thinking two French braids would look best with my tiara," I said. I put the tiara on. "What do you think?"

Grandpa looked me over, very serious-like. "I agree. Two braids is best."

When Emmeline came downstairs with Mom, she was wearing her red dress with the navy blue jacket, almost the exact same as mine. I opened my mouth to yell. And then she said, "Clara Lee, when I'm in third grade, I want to be Little Miss Apple Pie just like you."

Mom said, "You girls look adorable."

I closed my mouth and sighed. So what if we were wearing almost the exact same dress? It was Apple Blossom Festival, and I was Little Miss Apple Pie, and that was plenty good enough.

❀ ❀ ❀ ❀

My family dropped me off at the floats, and they said they'd be standing near Cooper's Drugstore, and to be sure to wave extra hard. Emmeline said I should throw her extra candy, and I said I would. Grandpa said to stand tall.

I climbed up the float, careful not to scratch my red tights. Miss Apple Pie was there wearing a long red dress, and it was silky. Her hair looked stiff, like she'd used a whole can of hair spray, and boy, was her apple tiara beautiful up close. "Hi there," she said. "So you're my little helper."

I felt shy all of a sudden. I wasn't used to hanging out with high school girls and adults. The mayor was on the float too; he was up front fixing the banner. "Uh-huh," I said.

"I love your dress," she said. "Where did you get it?"

I smoothed the skirt proudly. "My grandpa bought it for me in Korea."

"Wow! I've barely even left Bramley," she said, and I could tell she was really impressed and not just pretending to be impressed because I was a kid. "That's very cool."

I smiled big and held out my hand. "I'm Clara Lee, American as apple pie."